How Animals Communicate

Annette Smith

Contents

Animal Senses

Animals communicate through their senses for survival. They use their senses to find food and water, inform others, attract a mate and scare predators.

Animals send signals or messages to other animals or groups of animals, of the same or different species, through smell, sound, sight and touch.

A strong scent can attract other animals. A loud piercing sound or a bright colour can frighten predators away from a specific area. A caressing touch from a female can help her young feel safe and secure.

Animals of different species are able to share a water source by communicating that they mean no harm to the others.

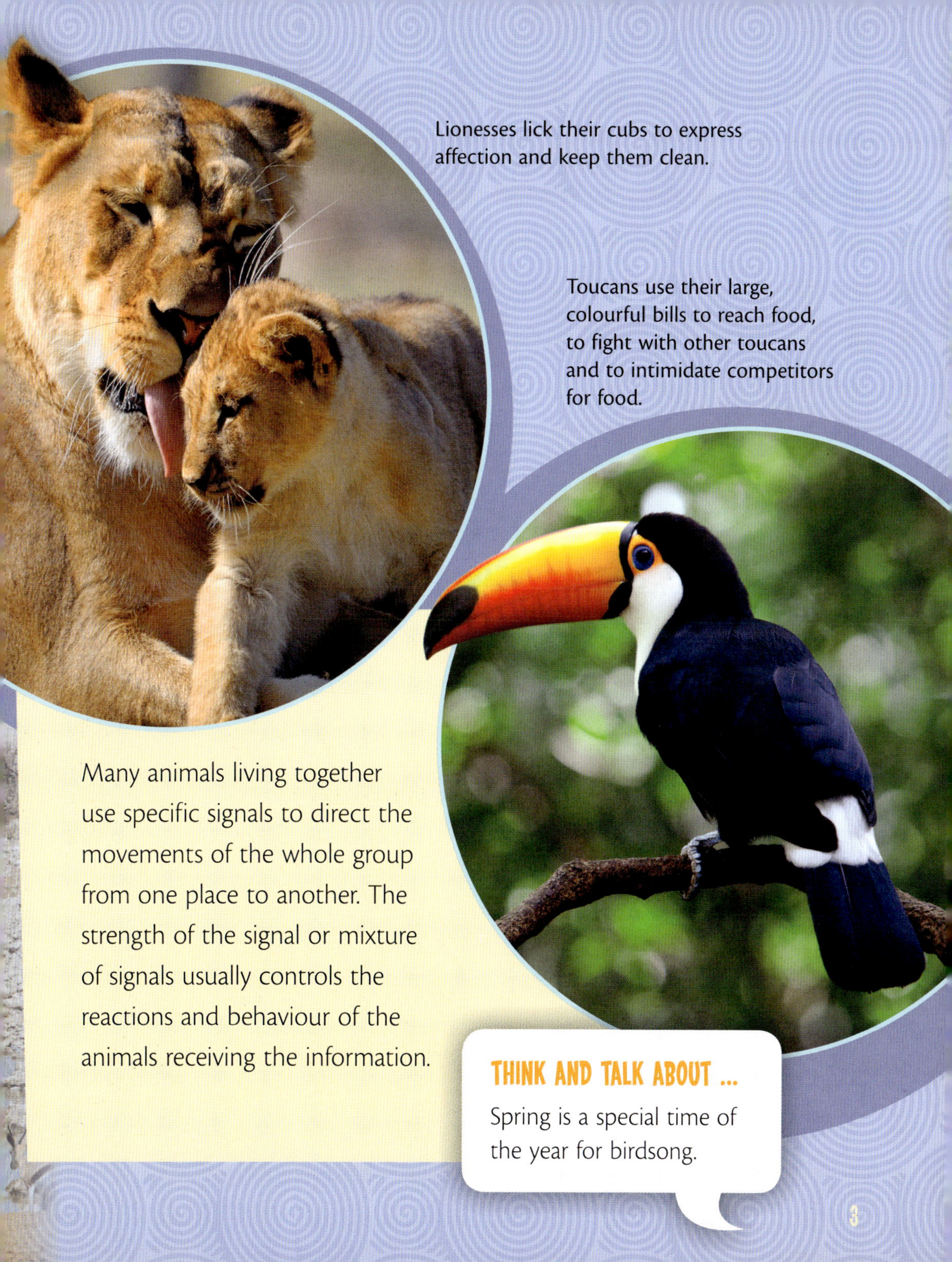

Lionesses lick their cubs to express affection and keep them clean.

Toucans use their large, colourful bills to reach food, to fight with other toucans and to intimidate competitors for food.

Many animals living together use specific signals to direct the movements of the whole group from one place to another. The strength of the signal or mixture of signals usually controls the reactions and behaviour of the animals receiving the information.

THINK AND TALK ABOUT ...

Spring is a special time of the year for birdsong.

Scent

Sharks' nostrils are used only for detecting scent; they breathe through the gills on the sides of their body.

Animal communication through the sense of smell is very common. Some animals and insects produce strong scents called **pheromones**. When a pheromone is released, it can change the behaviour of nearby animals of the same species.

Sharks have a very effective sense of smell. Some species of shark can even detect drops of blood in the ocean, indicating a wounded prey that can be easily overpowered. A shark has two nostrils, called nares, on the underside of its snout. Water continually flows through the nostrils into a nasal chamber. A shark does not breathe air through its nostrils.

Snakes have an unusual means of identifying scents in the air. A snake flicks out its tongue, then brings it back to touch a special **gland** in the roof of its mouth.

Some animals, such as hippopotamuses, leave large piles of droppings to mark their territory. Dogs spray urine as a warning to other dogs to stay away from a particular area.

Unlike most other animals, snakes "taste" the air to detect scents.

Ant Trails

Ants **evolved** on Earth more than 100 million years ago. They live in colonies made up of the queen ant and her workers. These workers include soldier ants that guard the queen, and hunter ants that search for food to bring back to the nest.

Ants communicate with each other using pheromones as signals. They use their long, thin **antennae** to identify the scent. The antennae provide the hunter ants with information such as the direction and quantity of a food source.

Ant colonies can range from hundreds to millions of ants.

When hunter ants find food, they mark their trails with pheromones on the way back to the colony. Other ants follow these trails and also mark them with similar pheromones as they return with food. Once the food supply has been reduced, no further scents are added to the trails.

THINK AND TALK ABOUT ...

Ants communicate with each other to solve difficult problems.

Sound

Some animals communicate by sound, because noise can travel very quickly over long distances. Sounds are useful because they can be heard during the day and night, and animals can change their volume depending on the conditions.

Marine animals rely on sound for communication. The speed of sound in water is far greater than on land.

A guard dog uses powerful signals, such as snarling angrily or barking loudly, when it detects an intruder nearby.

Shrill calls from a meerkat **sentry** warn other members of the community to escape immediately to the safety of underground dens.

Larger breeds of dog that look intimidating are often chosen as guard dogs.

Meerkat sentries are sent out alone to watch for predators.

The Caribbean White-lipped Frog is only found on a few islands in the Caribbean Sea.

The male Caribbean White-lipped Frog sings a range of chirps to attract a mate. When it sings, its throat sac swells and hits the ground, producing vibrations in the ground that can be felt by other males, so they know to keep their distance.

Grasshoppers and crickets create sound by rubbing their hind legs over the ribs, or ridges, on their wings.

THINK AND TALK ABOUT ...

Bats catch their food in the dark by using a special form of **sonar**.

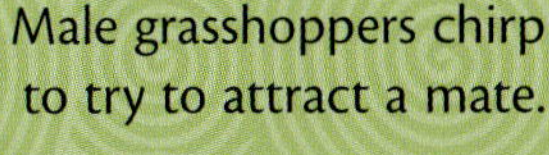

Male grasshoppers chirp to try to attract a mate.

The Whale's Song

Most whales travel in groups called pods. Whales are social animals and make a range of noises to let each other know where they are. The three main sounds made by whales are clicks, whistles and calls.

The clicking sounds are believed to help whales locate where they are and to identify objects close by. The sounds bounce back to them from the objects and from the sea floor. This is called echolocation.

When whales are working as a group, they use whistles and pulsating calls. Some calls sound like squeaks, screams or squawks. Many are too low or too high for humans to hear clearly. Each species of whale has its own special calls.

Humpback Whales sing the longest and strangest song of any animal. The song can last from 5 to 35 minutes. During this time, the sounds change from high squeaks to deep cries. The whale will often repeat the same song again and again for many hours, or even for several days. It is thought that male Humpback Whales sing to attract a mate.

THINK AND TALK ABOUT ...

The increase in shipping and use of sonar equipment is endangering many marine animals.

Humpback Whales often swim together in pods of 10 or more.

The Rattlesnake Shake

Rattlesnakes, found in North and South America, have developed a useful means of warning predators: the rattle. A Rattlesnake has hard rings of dry skin at the end of its tail. This skin is similar to the **keratin** that human nails are made of. Each time a Rattlesnake sheds its skin, it adds another section to the rattle. When the snake shakes its tail vigorously, the rings move and rub against each other to make a buzzing sound.

As well as rattling their tails, Rattlesnakes hiss to scare away potential predators.

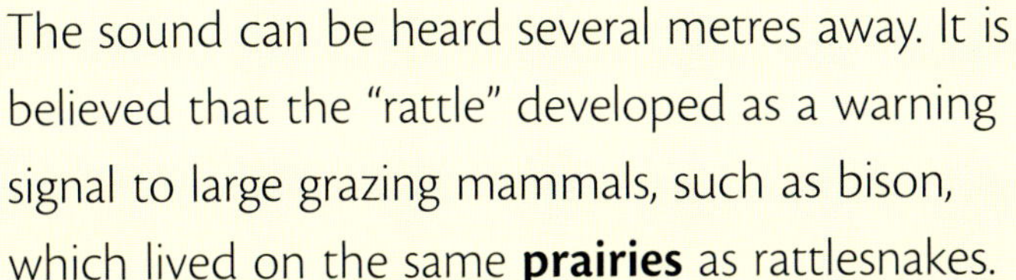

The sound can be heard several metres away. It is believed that the "rattle" developed as a warning signal to large grazing mammals, such as bison, which lived on the same **prairies** as rattlesnakes.

Kangaroo Rats stand upright and hop like kangaroos.

THINK AND TALK ABOUT ...

Kangaroo Rats use foot drumming to cause vibrations in the ground to scare away snakes.

Sight

The sense of sight is known as visual communication. Visual signals are most often used during the day, rather than at night-time. Many animals are awake during the day and can see these signals.

There are two forms of visual communication. The first type involves the colour, shape and size of the animal. The second type requires the animal to convey information through specific body actions and behaviour. These actions are sometimes referred to as a display or exhibition. Often, both forms of visual communication happen at the same time. A gorilla uses a range of facial expressions, including frowns, pouts and gazes, to express its feelings.

A peacock spreads his bright-green tail feathers into a gigantic fan to attract a mate. As he ruffles his feathers, his tail also makes a low-pitched sound.

Gorillas' facial expressions are often similar to humans'.

Only peacocks have brightly coloured tails; peahens are usually brown.

Frilled Lizards spread the flap of skin around their neck to try to intimidate predators.

If a Frilled Lizard is frightened, it will open its mouth wide and hiss loudly, showing its bright-yellow throat. Then, it suddenly spreads the flap of skin around its neck into a huge frill. To appear even more **menacing**, the lizard will stand upright on its hind legs, rocking from side to side and beating its tail on the ground.

Visual signals such as these have more impact if a predator or a mate is nearby.

Tarsiers are nocturnal, which means they are most active at night.

THINK AND TALK ABOUT ...

The tiny tarsier has enormous eyes that allow it to see in the dark.

The Dance of the Honey Bee

One of the most interesting forms of animal visual communication is the dance of the Honey Bee. The dance explains where food can be found, in relation to the hive.

Each female worker bee has to search vast areas and fly long distances to find nectar and pollen. When a new source of food is found, the bee returns to the hive, where she performs an extraordinary dance on the side of the honeycomb. She attracts the attention of other foraging workers, who immediately gather around her. Although the dance is performed in the darkness of the hive, it is understood by the others.

Part of the job of worker bees is to store pollen in the honeycomb.

The dance takes two distinct forms, depending on the distance and direction of the food source.

If the dancer performs the round dance, the others know that the food source is closer than 50 metres from the hive. First, the bee dances in small circles, and then turns and dances in the other direction for a few **revolutions**. This is repeated several times.

The waggle dance, or figure-of-eight dance, is performed by bees that have discovered sources of nectar and pollen further than 150 metres from the hive. The dancer runs straight ahead along the honeycomb for a short distance, then returns to the starting point in the shape of a semi-circle. Then, she runs up the straight line again but this time returns in a semi-circle in the opposite direction. While the bee is moving along the line between the two semi-circles, her **abdomen** waggles vigorously from side to side. At the same time, her wings are making a buzzing sound.

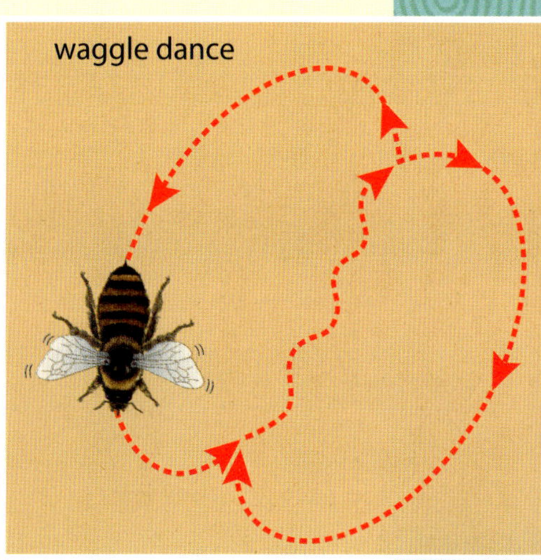

The dance of the Honey Bee takes two different forms.

The speed and angle of the waggle dance and the number of times it is repeated indicate the direction and distance of the food source.

The Crab Wave

Fiddler Crabs are small crabs found in burrows near the water's edge on sea beaches, as well as in lagoons, swamps and **inter-tidal** mudflats. These crabs often live together in large clusters.

Male Fiddler Crabs have one claw larger than the other. The females' claws are both the same size.

During summer, before mating, the male crab digs a burrow in the shape of a cylinder. He carefully protects his burrow as he waits for a female crab to walk past. When he sees one, the male crab waves his large pink-and-yellow claw to attract her attention. He runs towards her and then back to his burrow. He may repeat this several times, until the female either follows him to the burrow or moves away.

A group of crabs is sometimes called a "cast".

A lot of fighting occurs among the males as they attempt to protect their territories. If a male Fiddler Crab loses his large claw in a fight, the small claw on the opposite side will begin to grow larger the next time the crab moults. The new shells are soft after moulting, so the crab has to be **vigilant**. He hides away until his new shell hardens.

Male Fiddler Crabs wave their large claw as a form of visual communication.

Touch

Many animals use the sense of touch to convey their feelings to other animals of the same or different species.

Touch plays an important role when rivals challenge each other to a fight for the possession of food. The more **dominant** animal will often kill, wound or force the loser to retreat to a safer distance.

Some animals stroke and groom one another to form a bond. Monkeys and apes spend a large amount of time removing fleas, lice and other material from the fur of their mate or their young. This grooming is a sign of trust.

Monkeys are often very affectionate with each other.

Lion cubs learn how to hunt and fight by play-fighting with other cubs.

Play is a special form of behaviour by some young mammals. During play, the young learn the skills they will need later in life to react to a wide range of signals sent out by others.

Penguins survive in the fierce blizzards of Antarctica by gathering together in a tight huddle to keep warm and safe.

Emperor penguins take turns on the outside of the huddle so they can all share the warmth of the group.

THINK AND TALK ABOUT ...

Giraffes use their long necks in fierce battles to repel a challenger.

The Elephant Stomp

Elephants are very intelligent animals. They live in large herds and have many ways of communicating with those in their group, as well as other elephant herds.

Elephants experience emotions of love, grief, concern and curiosity, similar to humans. Touching and smelling each other with their trunks is an essential part of elephants living together as a social group. They use their trunks to stroke each other and to explore objects.

Mothers are often seen caressing their calves with their trunks. Elephants will engage in touching the face, ears or trunk of another elephant that appears to be feeling unsure about a situation.

If an elephant has been injured, other members of the herd will attempt to carry or lift it with their trunk or tusks.

Elephant mothers use their trunks to help their calves climb out of difficult places.

The position of the trunk is a sign of communication, too. When a male elephant lifts his trunk, it is a threat to another male. When the trunk is in a downward position, it is a sign of friendliness.

The **matriarch** of the family group plays an important role. If she needs the group to leave an area, she lifts or swings her foot in the direction she wants them to travel. These movements are accompanied by low, rumbling calls to the others to join her.

Elephants often communicate through vibration. They stomp their large feet when they sense danger. This vibration can travel many kilometres along the ground as a warning to other elephants.

As well as indicating friendliness, a lowered trunk can be a sign of sadness.

A raised trunk is often a sign of aggression.

THINK AND TALK ABOUT ...

Elephants detect **seismic** waves with the skin of their feet and trunk.

Communication for a Purpose

Communication is necessary for living creatures to exist. The "sender" conveys information to the "receiver" using a specific signal or a combination of signals. This information has many purposes.

The signal could be related to the discovery of food and water or the protection of this source.

A sender may defend a mate or a territory through angry signals to the receiver.

Alternatively, a **docile** response from one animal to another could send a completely different message.

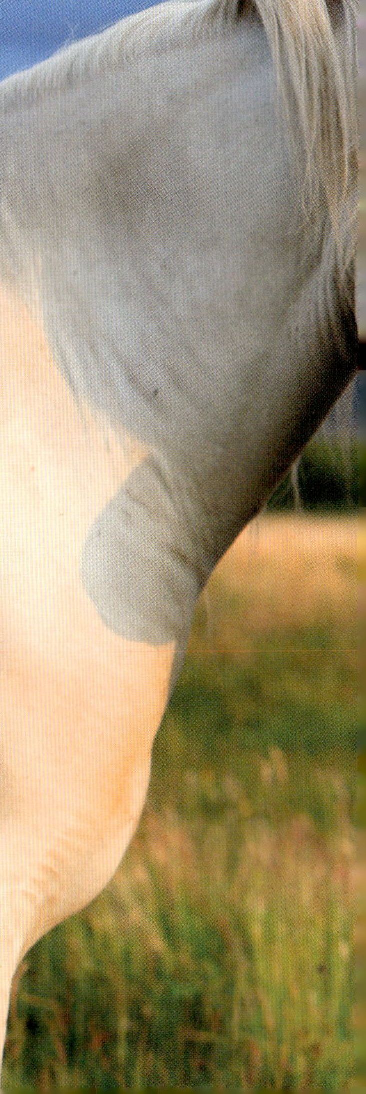

Mares and foals show affection by nuzzling each other and nickering softly.

Arctic wolves' howls can be heard up to 5 kilometres away.

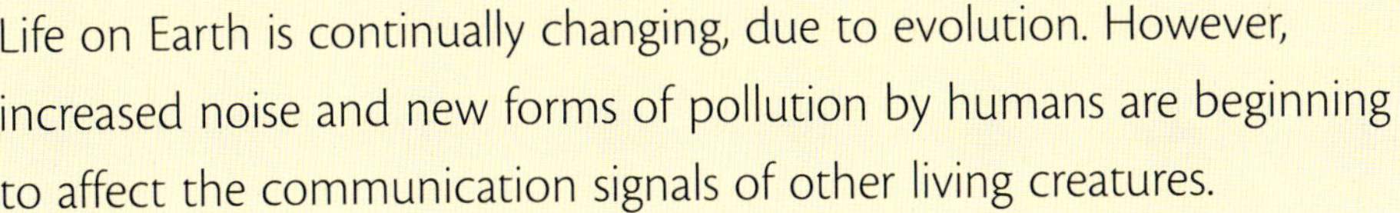

Life on Earth is continually changing, due to evolution. However, increased noise and new forms of pollution by humans are beginning to affect the communication signals of other living creatures.

Starlings sometimes fight over the best breeding sites.

THINK AND TALK ABOUT ...

Immediately prior to an earthquake or tidal wave, many animals within the same location become very still and quiet.

How Humans Train Young Working Dogs

Dogs are often referred to as "man's best friend". Dogs are used by humans in many ways, including for search and rescue, as guide dogs and for farm work.

A working dog usually has only one handler who is responsible for teaching it the skills required to fulfil the particular task.

First, the handler selects the breed of dog that will suit the situation in which it will be working. Search-and-rescue dogs working in snowy, mountainous conditions need to be extremely strong. The large St Bernard breed is well suited to these harsh situations. Labradors make excellent guide dogs because they are gentle animals. Farmers often choose Border Collies to herd sheep from difficult hilly sites. This breed of dog learns new jobs quickly and likes to please its master.

St Bernards are often chosen as rescue dogs in the Swiss Alps.

The dogs chosen for each type of work need to be young and healthy. The handler also requires a dog that is intelligent and is comfortable around humans.

Guide dogs have to be trained from a very young age.

Border Collies have been used as sheep dogs for more than 100 years.

THINK AND TALK ABOUT ...

Dogs have an acute sense of smell.

Next, the handler begins training the young dog with the basic voice commands: sit and stay.

Young dogs have a lot of energy. They require daily exercise to keep fit and healthy, and to stimulate their brains. During these times, it is very important that the dog learns to respond instantly to the basic commands.

Reward for a successful response may be a small treat, a light pat or a positive word.

Rewarding puppies with treats and praise makes them want to repeat their good behaviour.

Walking on a lead is one of the first things a working dog needs to learn.

At these early stages of training, the young dog needs to experience real situations in which it will be working later. These experiences could be: guide dog puppies travelling in buses, search-and-rescue dogs finding a lost item, or sheep dogs learning to squeeze quickly through strong fences on a farm.

When guide dogs are fully trained, they are able to guide their owner around safely.

As the dog's skills improve, the handler will introduce additional voice commands and hand signals. Many farmers also use whistles.

The handler has to be calm, yet firm, so that the young dog is obedient and understands exactly what it is meant to do.

Farmers often whistle to sheep dogs when they are too far away to respond to a voice command.

If a young dog is trained correctly, then it will be reliable and will work hard for the handler.

Search-and-rescue dogs use their sense of smell to find people who might be trapped after a natural disaster.

Glossary

abdomen (*noun*)	the segment of an insect's body containing the stomach
antennae (*noun*)	long, thin feelers on an insect's head
docile (*adjective*)	calm, gentle
dominant (*adjective*)	stronger, more powerful
evolved (*verb*)	changed over a long period of time
gland (*noun*)	an organ in the body that sends chemicals to other parts of the body
inter-tidal (*adjective*)	appearing between high tides
keratin (*noun*)	the protein that forms hair, fingernails, feathers, hoofs, claws and horns
matriarch (*noun*)	the female head of a family
menacing (*adjective*)	scary, intimidating
pheromones (*noun*)	scents released by animals that affect the behaviour of nearby animals of the same species
prairies (*noun*)	areas of grassland
revolutions (*noun*)	rotations, circles
seismic (*adjective*)	vibrations under Earth's surface
sentry (*noun*)	guard or lookout
sonar (*adjective*)	an acronym for SOund Navigation And Ranging; the system by which sound waves are used to create an image of the ocean floor
vigilant (*adjective*)	careful, wary and alert

Index